The Yellow Bills

The Yellow Bills

Michelle McKenna

Illustrated by Steven Johnson

Matador
9 Priory Business Park,
Wistow Road, Kibworth Beauchamp,
Leicestershire. LE8 0RX
Tel: 0116 279 2299
Email: books@troubador.co.uk
Web: www.troubador.co.uk/matador
Twitter: @matadorbooks

ISBN 978 1788036 610

British Library Cataloguing in Publication Data.
A catalogue record for this book is available from the British Library.

Printed and bound by CPI Group (UK) Ltd, Croydon, CR0 4YY
Typeset in 12pt Minion Pro by Troubador Publishing Ltd, Leicester, UK

Matador is an imprint of Troubador Publishing Ltd

This book is dedicated to my two little ducklings
Harry and Florence
May you be forever curious.

In Loving Memory of
Great Granny Betty

Thank you

When I embarked on this self-publishing journey I had the naive notion that all I needed to do was write a good story and upload it onto my website. As the story progressed I realised there are a number of people in your life who you need to help make it happen and I wanted to thank a few of those people here.

Karina at *mylittleduckling* for being brave enough to let me write a story about her pilot hat business. Ste Johnson for bringing my book to life with his beautiful illustrations and for re-introducing the word 'boss' back into my vocabulary. Dea at Fiction Feedback, I completely underestimated what a good copy-editor does. Thank you for helping me to polish the story off and introducing me to Uncle Puffin. Alison, Claire, Daniel, Carla, Edward and Theo for reading the drafts and giving me invaluable feedback. Mark for coming up with the title of the book (you now have that in print) and constantly encouraging me to keep going. To my mum, and sister Siobhan, who are two of the strongest women I know. Thanks for believing in me. And Dad, thanks for doing the gardening while I wrote.

Finally to all my friends and family a big thank you for your support.

Contents

Mya Meets Lieutenant Drake

Maps, atlases, globes. Mya wanted to see this glorious world from all angles. She may have been only eight years old but she knew without a doubt that she was going to be a pilot and see the world – just like her Uncle Arthur. He was a pilot for a big airline and whenever he came back to the UK he would bring her a gift from where he had been, along with a map of the area. Her bedroom walls were covered with these maps and on each one she stuck pictures of animals from that part of the world. Her favourite map was of Botswana in Africa, which had a picture of an elephant that her uncle had photographed while in the Okavango Delta.

Mya had hazel eyes that stood out against her dark olive skin, skin she inherited from her dad as well as the dark brown tight curly hair that bounced against her shoulders. Her mum who had straight red hair struggled to tame Mya's hair every morning. She usually gave up after a minute or so because of Mya's wriggling. Mya didn't care how unruly her hair was or wasn't. All she cared about was making

1

sure she was wearing her favourite purple Converse trainers and getting out to the garden to build her model aeroplanes.

She had finished her Spitfire and Merlin. Now she was going to start work on something more modern, a Hawk, the kind that flew in the Red Arrows. She had to build them in the shed at the bottom of the garden because her mum said glue and paint could get on the furniture.

She loved the anticipation of opening a new kit box. She carefully laid out the pieces, making sure not to cut them from the plastic sprue they were attached to until she was ready. She read that she was meant to paint detail such as the inside of the cockpit first and then assemble them, but this time she was too impatient and decided to put the plane together first and then paint.

"Red One, are you ready to fly?" She separated the main body of the plane and the cockpit from the sprue and carefully put them together. Taking one of her elastic bands she used it to hold the parts in place while the glue dried and then gently put the plane back on the bench.

"Attention!"

Mya stopped abruptly at the strange voice that had shouted. She looked around to see who was there. But the garden seemed empty, which was odd as the call had sounded very close.

"Get in line, Goose and Plum Sauce. You are

breaking the formation. If you do that in the air you could cause your fellow classmates serious problems."

Formation? In the air? This sounds fun, thought Mya. She crept outside the shed and searched all the bushes at the end of the garden as quietly as she could. Perhaps they were hiding there. Then she heard a distant shout of "left, right, left, right," and hunted further through the bushes, until she reached a hedge that was beyond her own garden. Her mum wouldn't be happy that she'd gone this far but she figured she wouldn't be long and would be back before Mum noticed.

She pushed her way through the bushes but they became thicker and sharper as thorns and twigs scratched at her arms and pulled on her hair, slowing her down and forcing her to wriggle through on her tummy. The voice became clearer and louder and she heard marching feet – then what sounded like a whole troop stamping their feet down.

"Now, what is the first rule of Little Duckling Flying School?" shouted the voice.

"Check the flight path is clear," responded a group of what sounded like children.

Flying school? thought Mya as she stopped crawling. Brilliant! Maybe I can join too.

"Second and third rules?" continued the voice.

"Check feathers and feet before take-off," shouted the young voices eagerly.

Mya giggled at the silly response, but stopped when she heard the teacher saying, "Correct."

Mya decided it was time to see what this was all about so she pushed herself up and through the hedge that was now in front of her. It opened out on to a small space surrounded by flowers and hedges, creating the perfect site for a private class. Mya brushed herself down and tried to remove the twigs that were tangled in her hair. The group were startled by her intrusion, but not as startled as she was. She stopped pulling out the twigs and they instantly moved out of the V formation they'd been standing in and flapped around to hide behind the teacher. He was also surprised, but puffed out his chest and stood his ground.

"How dare you interrupt my class? What do you think you are doing here? This is a restricted area." It was the same voice that Mya had heard before, but he didn't look anything like the teacher she'd imagined.

"Well?" shouted the teacher. "Do you know how to speak?"

Mya was lost for words but finally managed to open her mouth and spoke. "Yes I do. But how is it that you can?"

"What? Of course I speak. How else could I teach this class?" He pointed to all the pupils cowering behind him.

"Yes …" Mya hesitated to say the rest of the sentence, but she needed to state the obvious. "But you are a duck and they are ducklings."

4

"A duck! How dare you? I'm a drake and a lieutenant. Just you remember that. Now if you could just move along I need to finish my class. I don't have time for this nonsense, the clock is against us."

Mya wanted to challenge him more but she could only focus on how majestic he looked. His orange webbed feet looked strong and sturdy while there was a softness to the light brown feathers on his wings. He had a white ring of feathers around his neck and dark brown feathers on his plumage that he still stuck out at her. As she continued to look at him she noticed how his yellow beak shone in the sun and what she could see of his head was covered in beautiful iridescent green feathers. However the most impressive thing about the lieutenant was what he was wearing. He had what looked like a pilot's hat on his head. It was khaki green on the outside with goggles stitched on top. Flaps on the side of his head covered his ear holes. Mya could just make out a beautiful bright red lining beneath one of the ear flaps.

5

"Where did you get your hat from?" Mya asked, pointing at his head and forgetting all about the oddness of the situation. "I'd love to get one of those for myself."

"Get one?" Lieutenant Drake said incredulously. "You can't just get one. It has to be earned."

"Oh, that's great as I don't have money anyway. How do I earn one?"

Lieutenant Drake was now the one who was momentarily lost for words. He looked at Mya and couldn't believe what she was asking.

"YOU don't earn one. This is a very special pilot hat that can only be presented to the best flyers. And that does not include you. It's for us mallards when we graduate from flying school."

"Okay. Can I join your class then?" Mya asked Lieutenant Drake.

"What? Join our flying school?" Lieutenant Drake was flapping his wings vigorously and talking very fast. All the little ducklings behind him also flapped in a panic as they tried to move further back and out of his way. "It's called the Little Duckling Flying School, not the Little Human Flying School. Every duck knows, GIRLS AND BOYS DON'T FLY. I won't have you making a mockery of my school. This is for serious pupils with flying skills."

He pointed at Mya with one of his wings. "Where are your feathers? And how can you expect to fly safely when both of your eyes are on the front of your face? That's just to start with."

Lieutenant Drake had stung Mya's heart. She tried to ignore his anger and harsh comments but she couldn't stop her cheeks from burning up. She wanted to shout back but could feel the tears coming to her eyes. So she turned round and charged headlong through the bushes and back into her garden instead.

As she ran back in to the shed she swiped the Red Arrow off the bench in anger. The cockpit and body she had so painstakingly attached broke apart and Mya cried even more. She fell to the floor and covered her face with her hands while she bawled.

She was so busy being upset she didn't hear the small voice behind her trying to get her attention.

"Excuse me. Umm … Little girl. Hello. Hey. Stop crying."

What was that squeak? Mya turned round to where the voice was coming from and couldn't see anyone. Then she looked down and saw a small duckling with a mop of unruly feathers on top of his head – not unlike her own hair, she thought. The rest of his body was fluffy yellow with flecks of brown feathers on his chest and wings and he had a slate-grey beak. The webbed feet were much smaller than Lieutenant Drake's and a slate grey instead of his vivid orange.

"Leave me alone," she snapped at the little duckling, putting her head back in her hands. She wanted to sob more but the owner of the little voice wasn't leaving.

"I just wanted to say that I think you were very

7

brave to stand up to Lieutenant Drake. And I don't think he's right. You should be allowed to attend the class." He paused as if waiting to see if Mya would say anything. She didn't but her shoulders had stopped shaking and she didn't seem to be crying any more. "I could help," he continued.

That got Mya's attention.

Mya lifted her head to look at the little duckling. Her usually vibrant, hazel eyes were red-rimmed and her cheeks were wet.

"Help? How? You heard him. He won't let me join the class."

"Well … he doesn't need to know you're in the class. You could just hide in the back and listen from there," he said, trailing off as he lost confidence in his own plan. Then he had another thought. "Or I could teach you," he said gleefully.

"But you don't know how to fly either. How can I learn from you?" Mya replied, her voice low and sad.

He looked offended that Mya hadn't jumped at the idea, but carried on. "I'll go to the class in the morning and we can meet up in the afternoon, and I'll show you what we've learnt. All classes are nine to eleven in the morning and then I'm free to practise flying for the rest of the day."

"Hmm, I'm not sure." Mya looked at the little duckling whose eyes pleaded with her as they appeared to grow bigger. Her gaze was caught by the metal mobile above him that her mum had hung from the tree the previous summer. It spun in the light breeze, creating an illusion that the bird painted in the centre was flapping its wings and flying. And the crystals on the end caught the light and gave off shards of rainbow colours that bounced on the ground and on to the little duckling's body. She'd always found it magical to watch and now she felt sure that it was there to help her make a decision. A decision not to be defeated by mean Lieutenant Drake. A decision to prove him and the other ducks wrong. Girls and boys really can fly and earn their pilot hats.

"Okay. I'll do it." Mya jumped up and startled the little duckling, who instinctively flapped his wings and ran into the closest bush before settling down and edging his way back into the garden. "Sorry, I didn't mean to scare you. What's your name?"

He puffed out his chest and proudly said, "Goose."

Mya laughed but quickly put on a straight face as she could see Goose wasn't happy. "So, Goose, have you always been called Goose even though you're a duckling?"

"Goose is my call sign. We're all given pilot names and I wanted to be known as Goose because I'm going to be the fastest drake in the sky," he replied with delight shining in his eyes.

"Oh I see. I like it," said Mya not knowing whether geese could fly fast or not. "I need a call sign too. What can I be called? Hmm … How about Reds, like the Red Arrow plane I'm painting?" She pointed to the plane smashed on the floor and was painfully reminded of what she had broken. And dismissed the thought instantly. "Actually how about—"

"I was thinking you could be called Star Catcher," said Goose, "like the star on your feet. It was the first thing I noticed about you."

Mya looked down at her favourite purple Converse trainers and looked at the star printed on it. She pondered. "Yes, that's perfect! Star Catcher it is."

"Star Catcher, I have to go now. See you here tomorrow at four for our first class." Goose flapped his wings and waddled quickly towards the bushes and disappeared before Mya had a chance to thank him.

Just then Mya's mum came out to the garden.

"Mya, is everything okay? I thought I heard you crying. And was that a little duckling I saw?"

Mya smiled and turned around to face her mum. "Everything is great, Mum. I'm going to be a pilot but I need to start training." With that she headed back to the shed to come up with a plan.

Mya's mum looked confused but not surprised as she always thought her daughter had a good imagination.

"Okay. Well, training will have to be put on pause in thirty minute's time. I've got you some lunch. See you in the house then."

Flying School

Mya paced up and down the garden as she waited for Goose to arrive. She had been working on her plan all afternoon and now she was keen to try it. Her mum was busy in the house sewing costumes for the local theatre company and thought Mya was working in the shed.

"What's in the bag?" Goose asked as he came up behind Mya. Mya jumped a little from the shock but soon recovered.

"My secret weapon."

Goose was going to ask more questions but knew they had very little time so decided he'd find out later. "Okay, let's go."

Mya followed Goose through the bushes. There was no ducking for Goose but plenty of it for Mya as she tried to negotiate her way through the undergrowth. She'd never ventured this far from her home on her own and couldn't believe how many shrubs there were. She'd always thought it was a few trees at the end of the garden and then more houses at the back of that. But now the path was twisting and winding through thorny, prickly bushes that her bag kept catching on. The friendly flowers and soft petals of her garden had long disappeared.

It seemed like an eternity to Mya, but it was really only about ten minutes before Goose stopped and turned around. "We're here, but keep low as we don't want the others seeing you."

"Others?" Mya peered through the gap that Goose had run through and saw she was in the woods. There were great big tall trees towering over them and smaller ones that looked a little more homely. Well, homely for those with feathers. It was buzzing with wildlife, like an avian metropolis. There were swans flying above and swallows zipping in and out of the trees while three red kites glided high above in what looked like a beautiful dance as they circled each other in a figure of eight. Just below them Mya saw a young pigeon on one of the branches concentrating very hard on the three pigeons below him on the ground. She thought he was just watching them but then realised he was aiming. A poop fell straight on to one of the pigeons. They seemed to recognise him as they squawked in anger and flew up after him and chased him through the trees.

Just then a familiar duck caught Mya's attention. Lieutenant Drake was marching along with a line of ducks behind him who were older than Goose and all wearing an array of the pilot hats that Mya so desperately wanted. One of the mallards had a purple and yellow floral hat and another had a navy blue one with stars printed on it and wonderful red goggles stitched on top.

"They're the best of the best flyers," Goose whispered into Mya's ear. "Once you get your pilot hat you can carry on flying or you can train to be in the elite squad that performs for us in the summer."

Mya got all excited. "You mean like the Red Arrows?"

Goose looked confused. "No. The Yellow Bills."

Mya watched as the squad marched into a doorway carved into the bottom of a tree. They look amazing, Mya thought wistfully, and I haven't even seen them fly.

"That's where we are going." Goose pointed to the tree that the Yellow Bills had just passed into. "It's the Control Tower. It's where all the air traffic is controlled from and where our classes begin."

"You have air traffic control?" Mya said, astounded.

"Of course. How else can we have this much flying going on and no crashes? We haven't had a crash here since we set up the tower five years ago."

"Hmm. I didn't think birds would need traffic control. I thought you just knew," Mya murmured to the sky without expecting an answer, let alone a logical one. She realised now that anything was possible. Except getting to the Control Tower without being detected. The ground and skies were busy and she would be very exposed as soon as she ran into the clearing. The Control Tower itself had a massive circumference to its base and was by far the biggest of all the trees there. As her eyes followed its trunk towards the sky she noticed how it was heavily covered by leaves but behind them, there appeared to be clusters of oval-shaped bushes dotted along the branches of the tree. She was keen to get over there to know what they were.

"Goose, how are we going to get over there without any of these birds seeing me?"

Goose put his wing to his beak to signal she should be quiet. Then he whispered, "Five, four, three, two, one." And with that there wasn't a bird to be seen. They had dived into one of the cosy-looking homes, flown out of sight or disappeared high into the tree tops. "It's teatime," said Goose.

"Of course it is," responded Mya.

Goose picked up on her sarcasm. "We all need to have a break and it's important we take this with friends or family."

"Won't anyone notice you aren't there for tea?"

"Well, I told Mum I was with Plum Sauce and Plum said she'd cover for me. Good plan, eh?"

"Yes, that is good. I'll remember that one for myself. Mum would never suspect a thing."

"Come on, we have to go now – we have less than an hour." They darted across the open space and ran straight for the Control Tower door. A large brown door, it was camouflaged so well Mya would never have found it on her own. Goose stuck his beak through one of the numerous small gaps sliced into the right of the door. He held his head in the same position for a few seconds, pulled back and the door swung open.

Mya whispered. "What was that?"

"It's a beak scanner. You stick your beak through the reader and it scans to make sure you have security clearance. Unfortunately I only have clearance for the training floor on level two but I'm hoping to get access to level nine someday. That's where they train the Yellow Bills."

The hallway they'd arrived in smelt woody and on the walls there were huge carvings of birds. To the right was a carving of nine ducks in mid-flight. The display formed a diamond shape. To the left was a painted portrait of a mallard that Mya couldn't drag her eyes from. Even though the hallway was dark there were well-positioned small holes throughout the tree that let light shine though like skylights and some shone brightly on this painting. It made the brown and caramel-coloured feathers look as if this duck was sparkling. The yellow bill was almost gold and the duck's stance made her look proud, tall and ready to take anything on. She was wearing an officer's hat and one of the wings was outstretched. The legs were long and sturdy. Mya looked again. Actually it wasn't legs; it was one leg with the webbed foot planted to the ground taking all the weight.

"Star Catcher, come on, we need to get to level two quickly," Goose snapped – then paused when he saw what was holding her up. "It's a great picture, isn't it? One of my favourites."

"It is, but the artist has forgotten to put in the other leg."

"The other leg? Don't be silly, Officer Peacock only has one leg. She is our first Yellow Bill without two legs."

"Why does she only have one leg?"

"She was born that way. The story goes that she used to get teased a lot as a little duckling by classmates and some of the parents. They used to call her the lame duck and said she'd never amount to anything so there was no point in joining the flying school as she would hold the other ducklings back. Many thought it was best she just stayed with her parents to be looked after."

"What did she do?"

"Well, my Uncle Puffin told me that at first Officer Peacock believed everyone. Then Lieutenant Drake flew to her home one day and bluntly told her that every duckling must attend his class and unless they were on their sickbed he wouldn't take no for an answer. Uncle Puffin said when he saw Officer

Peacock turn up at class she looked quite scruffy, as she'd ruffled the feathers on her head so much they covered her eyes. She told him later she did that so she couldn't see everyone's stares. He also said that while she'd become much better at hopping she found it difficult to get up the stairs to the classroom. She was so embarrassed, but Lieutenant Drake informed the class that it was time everyone started doing classes outside and that's when he set up an area like the one you saw the other day so that every duckling could access it."

"That was nice of him," Mya said, but then screwed up her face as she remembered it was Lieutenant Drake she was talking about.

"It was, but not everyone in the class was happy as it meant a lot of days in the rain as well as the sun. She wasn't very popular. Uncle Puffin said her classmates would try to nudge her so she'd lose her balance and fall over. But she was determined to be the best and she would practise her hopping whenever she could so her leg got stronger. Eventually she was the bee's knees, or as I like to say, the duck's quack, at jumping up the stairs and could reach the classroom quite easily. By then her wings had got stronger and when everyone else was playing, she kept hopping and flapping and managed to be first in the class to take off. She was so good that Lieutenant Drake let her take the exam early, which she passed, and he said she should go for the Yellow Bills."

Goose paused and looked around. "Quick, someone's coming. Hide." With that, he sprinted to a door under the stairs. Mya panicked as the space Goose was hiding in was too small for her. She clattered up the stairs until she got to the first level and found a door to open. It was a small broom cupboard, filled with brushes and buckets, and it smelt awful. As soon as she closed the door she nearly ran back out but couldn't as she heard movement on the stairs. She left a small gap in the door so she could stick her nose out and get some cleaner air. It also meant that she was able to see who was coming up the steps. There were two swans dashing up them, squawking at each other.

"I told you we didn't have time to eat that bread in the river, didn't I?"

"How was I to know that the child would take so long to get the bread out of the bag?"

"It's not just that, it was those pesky geese and seagulls surrounding us. I can't believe we had to fight them just to get some crusts when the child was clearly trying to feed us. How dare they muscle in on our patch? We are the most graceful birds there and should be top of the pecking order. A little more manners is what is needed on that river. I'll have to spend the afternoon cleaning my feathers now."

They continued to moan at each other as they clambered up the stairs.

Mya had never heard such complete snobs but was happy they were in a rush. As soon as they passed she fell out of the door and on to her knees just to gulp in some air. She got up and shouted in a loud whisper down the stairs, "Goose? Goose? I think we're good to go." Then she heard a little patter as Goose tried to run up the stairs. His feathers looked more unruly than normal.

"That was close," he panted, and looked at Mya. "What happened to you? You look green." Before Mya could answer he looked at the open door behind her. "Oh, you hid in there. Sorry. That's the kit for cleaning out the nests. Some of the birds have accommodation in the control tower and if you're unlucky enough to get detention the teachers make you help with cleaning them out. Don't worry, the smell goes after a while." Mya just nodded as she held her nose and hoped he was right.

"I wasn't expecting to see anyone. We have to be super careful. C'mon, follow me to the training room and no stopping this time."

They arrived on the second floor which had a very narrow corridor and an arched doorway at the end. Mya guessed this must be the entrance to one of the big cluster of bushes she'd seen outside, except she could see now that these clusters were actually rooms. The doorway was just about big enough for Mya and she was pleased the place inside was big enough to accommodate human children.

In the room was a blackboard on one wall and a smartboard on another. She walked over to the smartboard on the right hand side. It had arrows highlighting the direction of the wind and the speed at which it was good to fly. There was even a section on dietary requirements and how it wasn't safe to eat baked beans before a flight unless you were an experienced flyer, as the extra wind would make you go faster.

"The take-off and landing are the hardest parts," Goose said behind Mya. "We've been learning what the best weather conditions are to fly in and the most dangerous. Let's put it this way; if it rains heavy I'm staying indoors."

"Rain? I thought ducks liked water."

"I do, but I don't want to fly in it. And don't even get me started on flying in lightning. My Uncle Puffin said he knows of a duck who ignored the flight safety rules and got struck by lightning. Ever since then he's only been able to fly backwards."

"Backwards? That can't be helpful?"

"It's not. Although it would be good to have him in front of you on a flight as he can tell you if anything is about to overtake you. He'd be like a talking rear view mirror." Goose chuckled.

"And what is this?" Mya pointed to the blackboard at the end of the room. It had squiggles she couldn't decipher that seemed to form a V shape.

"They're the names of everyone in the class and the positions we should take in the air. At the moment we've just been practising in here and the spot you saw us yesterday, so we can get used to knowing where everyone should be in the sky. I have Plum Sauce in front of me and Tails behind me. Once we can get in the air we have to stay in these positions whenever we fly for a few days. Then we go out on a test flight on our own with Officer Peacock and she tells us if we're ready to take the final test.

Mya studied the blackboard and was fascinated that the class had to fly as a team by keeping their position and creating the V shape in the air. She realised this class wasn't just about flying, but flying in style.

"Okay. Right, let's start. Stand up straight. Shake out those feathers. Um, sorry, I mean shake out your arms and legs." Mya did as she was told and stood on the spot, jiggling her arms and legs.

"Good. Move your head from side to side and stretch those neck muscles. Now, stand straight again and stretch out your wings. I mean arms. Move them up and down slowly first, like this." Goose moved his wings up and down very slowly and gradually got faster and faster until he built up enough momentum to push the air around him and get enough lift so he was six inches off the ground. He hovered for about twenty seconds, and then collapsed back on to the floor. "That's hard work," he said breathlessly. "You try."

"Wait a minute. Just let me get my secret weapon," Mya said as she bent down and pulled out what looked like a ball of feathers from her bag. She stretched them out – now they looked like a huge pair of wings. "I stole some of Mum's chicken wire that she was using for her costumes and thought I'd make some wings. I've glued all different feathers to them that I found in the garden. What do you think?"

The wings had a large span, but looked messy as there were clumps of feathers scattered across the chicken wire.

"Well, I think it's going to be a lot better than just using your arms. Good work, Star Catcher. Now let's get flapping."

Mya put her arms through the straps she had made so that the wings sat on her back. It didn't feel comfortable, but she could still move her arms up and down. She started off slowly, and then built up speed by moving them faster and faster. She went

on her tippy-toes to see if that would help, but no matter how hard she flapped nothing happened, except that she got redder and hotter. Goose looked on with concern as he realised that his first teaching job couldn't be any tougher.

Mya stopped. She stood there sulking, annoyed that her plan hadn't worked. "It's no good. Lieutenant Drake was right – I can't fly."

Goose tried to stay positive. "Don't give up. I know what to do. I think it would help if we went to the launch pad over here." He pointed to another arched door to the left of the room. He walked over and pushed it open. It led outside, but not to a nice terrace or rooftop garden. It was simply a huge thick branch surrounded by foliage above and below. Goose walked out confidently on to the branch and beckoned Mya to follow him. It was wide enough and strong enough to take her weight but it took Mya's breath away when she saw how high up they were. She crawled out on her hands and knees.

"Don't worry, it's only five metres high."

"Goose, if I can't get off the ground in there, how am I going to do it out here? Are you sure this is safe?"

"Star Catcher, you just need a bit of momentum. As you jump off, start flapping and the speed will help you."

"You mean the speed of falling will help me fall quicker?"

"Don't be silly. Look. Let me go first. It's not my favourite thing to do, I'll be honest, but it does help." And with that he dived off the launch pad. Unfortunately he opened his wings a little too late and plummeted towards the ground. He flapped furiously which slowed him down by a few milliseconds, but couldn't put off the inevitable. THUMP!

Mya looked down to where he was lying and squirmed at the painful landing. The duckling didn't move.

"Goose? Goose? Are you okay?"

With that Goose lifted himself up and stumbled a little, and then looked up at Mya.

"See, I made it. A bit of a shaky landing but practice makes perfect." He abruptly sat down. "I'm just waiting for the world to stop spinning. Once it has, it's your turn."

Feathers, glorious feathers

Mya cautiously raised herself to her full height on the branch, not knowing what to do next. This was not what she'd planned. The feathers were meant to work straight away. She wasn't convinced the 'momentum' Goose was talking about was going to help.

"No, it's no good. I'm taking the stairs," Mya said to herself and began to edge back to the classroom entrance.

But before she could reach the safety of the classroom, she was startled by a voice shouting from the branch below her. It was a duck who had poked its head out from another room and was looking round the tree.

"What's going on here?" the voice said as it waddled out on to the branch and looked down to see Goose rubbing his head. "Goose, what are you doing outside?"

"Mr Sour," Goose shrieked in surprise as he looked up.

Mya felt she was moving in slow motion as her body weight shifted too much to the left of the branch.

There was nothing for it, she was going to have to try and fly as she fell off. She went to flap her wings but instinctively grabbed at the duck below as she passed. She hoped against hope that he could take her weight and fly them both to safety.

He couldn't take her weight.

And because she had grabbed him round his body, his wings were pinned down so there was no way even for him to fly off on his own. It was a crash landing for both, but they did manage to land on a pile of foliage that softened the blow. As they hit the ground Mya let go of the duck and rolled on to her back to catch her breath.

Mr Sour flapped his wings to get his balance back and landed near to Mya. He was full of rage as he looked at her.

"What did you grab me for, you stupid girl? Look at me. I'm losing feathers. I'll be bald before the day is finished," exclaimed Mr Sour as he looked in dismay at the feathery chaos around him. There were feathers flying everywhere and settling on everything in sight. Goose almost disappeared underneath them. He shook them off, looked at Mr Sour and wished he'd stayed hidden.

Mr Sour checked his body all over to see where there might be bald patches. He was confused and relieved to see that every feather was in place, even if they were a little ruffled.

Mya observed that this duck looked like

Lieutenant Drake, in that he had the fluorescent green head, white collar and brown plumage feathers, but he wasn't wearing a pilot hat. He seemed scruffier and smaller than Lieutenant Drake but also plumper.

"Well, girl, do you have anything to say?" snapped Mr Sour.

Mya couldn't sit up yet so she stayed flat on her back but she couldn't help feeling she was in big trouble this time. It was as if one of her teachers were telling her off and as she'd never been in trouble before, she thought it best to tell the truth.

"I'm trying to fly."

"Fly? What do you mean fly?" replied Mr Sour, sounding very shocked. "You can't fly. You're a human."

"Yes, I seem to get told that a lot lately," Mya said in a disappointed tone. She was beginning to feel very silly for even thinking she could fly.

"Don't worry about the feathers, they're mine."

"What do you mean, your feathers?" Mr Sour looked at Mya properly as she lay sprawled on the ground, arms outstretched with chicken wire beneath her and a splattering of feathers all across. "Oh I see. Well you just keep confirming to me how stupid you are.

"And you." He quickly turned to Goose. "You still haven't answered me as to why you're out here."

Goose cowered but knew he should answer. "Sorry, Mr Sour, I was just practising my flying technique and thought now would be a good time while it's quiet."

"And the girl?" Mya was starting to get annoyed by this cranky duck called Mr Sour. She didn't like being talked about as if she wasn't there, but was too busy concentrating on the feathers blowing in the wind above her to complain. The fall had taken the stuffing out of her as well as the chicken-wire wings.

"Well, answer me, Goose, what about the girl? How did she manage to get past security and access the launch pad? You're aware of how serious this breach of security is, aren't you? If I find you've helped her you'll be mucking out the nests for the rest of the year." As he spoke he waddled over and poked his beak menacingly at Goose's small chest. Mya had lifted herself up on to her elbows and didn't like what she was seeing. This duck was a bully. She had to do something to take his attention away from Goose.

"Hey. I've no idea why you're nudging that duckling. I've never seen him before."

"Really?" Mr Sour turned round to Mya with a sneer as if he was looking forward to her explanation.

"So how come you were up there?" He pointed with his wing to the branch above.

"I love climbing trees."

"And you thought you'd climb this one?"

"Yes. I don't see a sign that says I can't."

"And you got all the way up there using just your hands and feet? Or did you use your feathers?" he commented sarcastically.

"Yep, just my hands and feet." Mya was beginning to get annoyed with all the questions. Also, she was never good at lying and he was bound to catch her out soon.

"Show me."

"What?"

"Show me how you climbed up there."

"I can't."

"You can't?" He grinned.

"Duh! Did you not notice I've just fallen and am a little shaken?"

Mr Sour's grin disappeared. "So, explain this to me. Why did I hear you shouting Goose's name before I looked out?"

"I saw a goose in the sky and just shouted out the name." Mya stumbled over the dishonest story, and knew she wasn't convincing. This duck was out-smarting her. It was exhausting. She stood up quickly so he couldn't quiz her further. A little too quickly, because she felt dizzy, but she was determined to get away from Mr Sour.

"Where are you going? I asked you a question," Mr Sour shouted at her as she made her way back to the bushes they had come through. "If I see you back here you'll be in big trouble, flying girl."

Mya carried on. In the distance she could hear Mr Sour shouting at Goose but couldn't make out what was being said. She wanted to go back and help but she had to keep pretending she didn't know Goose, so she hid in the bushes hoping he would come and find her. As she waited there she noticed the skies started to get busier with birds and she realised that teatime must be over. Goose wasn't going to be able to look for her now, so with a heavy heart she squeezed back through the bushes to her home, which was even more difficult this time as the chicken wire dragged her down and caught on every branch and thorn she passed. She wondered if she would ever see her new friend Goose again.

Missing in Action

It had been six days since Mya had seen Goose.

After she left him with Mr Sour, she managed to get home without her mum noticing she'd disappeared. But her mum did look concerned when she caught Mya in the garden looking as though she'd been dragged through a hedge backwards. Mya convinced her mum that she'd been practising flying out of one of the trees in the garden. And she didn't get too many questions after that. Just lots of pitying looks. However, her mum seemed to be keeping an eye on her in the garden a lot more since that day, presumably worried that Mya might try to jump out of a tree again. So even if Goose did turn up, Mya couldn't get away as easily.

She felt awful for leaving Goose. She wished she had stayed to defend her friend but was sure if she'd said any more it would have made it worse for him.

Now she decided to get her little backpack from the shed and go looking for him. It was worth the risk of being caught by her mum. She couldn't mope around any longer, she needed to do something.

As she was packing her bag she heard a rustle from the one of the bushes. Was it Goose? She hoped it was. She needed to know he was okay. She ran out, but was disappointed to see a little blackbird hopping on the branches. It flew off in an instant when it spotted Mya.

Mya let out a little sigh of disappointment and returned to the shed.

"How are your aeroplanes coming on?" Mya's mum poked her head around the door of the shed.

"Well, I've nearly painted half a plane," Mya fibbed as she moved the bag she was packing from her chair to under the work bench. She made herself look busy by moving one older, painted plane from one side of the bench to another.

"That's good," her mum responded, though Mya realised from her mother's expression she'd maybe not sounded as enthusiastic as usual. "Mya. You haven't been yourself for the last few days and when you told me how much you'd been working on a plan to fly, I thought I'd have a chat with some of the stage guys at the theatre company and we've come up with a little gift for you," she said excitedly. "Do you want to pop outside and I'll show you."

Mya dragged her heels as she dawdled out of the shed and into the garden. She looked up and was greeted with a confusing sight.

"What do you think?"

"What have you done to my bike?" Mya cried. Her

bike was still in one piece but now had two large yellow polystyrene pieces stuck together above it creating a large wing with stiffened leather straps coming down from it, which connected to the front and back wheels to keep it in place. Behind the wing there was a tail fin and propeller. It was enormous and Mya had no idea how she could be seen in the park with her bike now.

"Can't you tell? We've turned it into a flying bike."

"Really?" Mya wasn't sure what she was feeling now. She was mortified and intrigued all at the same time.

"Well, you've always wanted to be a pilot and when I saw you the other day with all those feathers clinging to your head and that chicken wire stuck to your back I realised how serious you are about flying."

"Oh wow. Thank you, Mum. How high can it get?"

Mya's mum laughed. "It doesn't actually fly."

Mya's face dropped.

"Don't be silly Mya, I wasn't going to get you something that might hurt you. This is so you can play at being a pilot. Now stop looking so grumpy and try it out."

Mya was livid at her mum for laughing at her. She'd show Mum she would make this bike fly. She got on the seat and looked up at the wing above her and the propeller behind her. This was exactly what she needed. She put her hands on the handlebars and focused on pedalling as hard as she could.

As she approached the end of the garden she realised the bike was a lot heavier to ride now that it had more weight attached to it. She started to brake but it took much longer to slow down and she went straight into a bush head first.

Do pilots really get hurt this much when learning to fly? Mya thought to herself, her head stuck through the shrub.

"Mya!" She heard her mum yelp from the top of the garden. Then she looked down and saw a familiar beak.

"Goose," she cried, then heard her mum running towards her. "Hang on." She pulled her head out of the bush and looked back at her mum. "Don't worry, I'm all good. I just need to get the hang of the braking distance."

Mya's mum looked relieved. "Thank goodness.

Okay, if you're sure you're all right I'll go and make us some lunch."

"Thanks, Mum, that'd be great. I'll just take it easy and do a bit more practising."

"It's good to see you happy again. Okay, I'll do some sandwiches. And I was thinking of doing roast duck for dinner tonight. Do you fancy that?"

Goose let out a little shriek from the bushes. Mya's stomach turned at the thought of it. "Mum, can I have something vegetarian, please?"

"Really? But I thought duck was your favourite?"

"Mum!" Mya squealed as she turned bright red. "I'm a vegetarian now. As of today."

"Okay. Cheese sandwiches it is. I'll think of something else for dinner."

Mya's mum walked back to the house and Mya crept through the bushes to see Goose.

She picked the duckling up and squeezed him tight. "Goose, I've missed you. What happened? I'm so sorry I left you with Mr Sour."

She put Goose down so he could speak.

"Roast duck!" he squeaked with a panicked look in his eye.

"What? … Oh. No, don't worry, Mum's not doing that now and I'll make sure we never eat anything with duck again. I promise! Now tell me what's happened to you. How did you get that cut on your face?" She could see scratches and scrapes on the right side of Goose's face and wing.

35

He was hesitant to speak.

"Goose, it's me. I promise I won't eat you. To be honest there isn't enough meat on you," she teased, but Goose was horrified and she quickly took the smirk off her face. "I'm joking."

He seemed reassured as he cautiously edged closer and gave Mya an update on what he'd been doing. "Plum and I had a collision in the air yesterday."

"You're flying? That's brilliant," Mya said, even though deep down she was a little bit jealous.

"Yes, I finally got to take off, four days ago. But Plum and I were so tired from all the work Mr Sour has got us doing as punishment, that we lost concentration and broke formation in the air. It got very ugly and the rest of the class weren't happy. I'm okay though."

"Surely Lieutenant Drake can't tell you off for that if old Sour Grapes is making you work?"

"Lieutenant Drake doesn't know. Mr Sour promised not to tell him anything if we cleaned all the nests for a week."

"But Plum wasn't involved!"

"He worked out that Plum had covered for me so we both got into big trouble." Goose saw how upset Mya looked. "But don't worry, we didn't say we'd helped you and because you pretended not to know me, he has no proof, so he punished us for lying to our parents about where I was. But we've finished our chores early today which is why I could finally come and see you."

"Mr Sour Pants is even more horrible than Lieutenant Drake."

"Yes, he stinks. My Uncle Puffin says he's just extra mean because he never made the Yellow Bills and Officer Peacock did. No one wants to be in his class though as he's always giving out detentions even for the smallest things like cleaning your feathers when he speaks to you. But enough about him. How are you? I'm sorry you never got to fly."

"I'm brilliant, and I think I've found a solution to my flying problem but I'm going to need a little help. Do you think you could get some of your friends to help cause a distraction?"

"Absolutely," Goose responded with enthusiasm.

"Great. Meet me here in thirty minutes with Plum Sauce and I'll let you know my plan."

"Mya, lunch is ready," her mum shouted from the patio door.

"Right, I'd better go," she said to Goose.

"I'll go and find Plum." Goose waddled quickly back towards the Control Tower. And Mya ran back to the house for her veggie sandwiches.

The Great Escape

"Charge!" cried the pigeon flying above Mya. It was the same one she had seen pooping on others at the Control Tower days before and she didn't like him. He was heading straight for the open patio door of her house at the top of the garden. Well, he thought it was open, but it wasn't, it was just very clean glass. BANG! He went head first into the door. Mya was relieved to see the pigeon was okay as it stumbled in the air but made a clean landing on the patio.

What have I done? she thought. It had seemed such a good idea in her head but now she wasn't so sure. True to their word, Goose and Plum Sauce had come back to meet her and she'd told them her plan. They'd arrived at eight on the dot this morning with Tails and the rest of their classmates. Mya only wanted the group of ducklings to move a few things in the house to keep her mum distracted while she moved the bike out of the garden. She wasn't expecting a couple of pigeons to join in. Goose had explained that they weren't invited but were bored. When they overheard the plan they wanted to "help".

Mya's mum came to the door to see what had happened and as soon as she opened it a squad of little ducklings sneaked in behind her while she examined the dazed pigeon on the patio. She ran back in after the ducklings once she spotted them to shoo them out, but another pigeon flew in and that's when things started to break and pictures fell off the wall.

Mya moved the bike from the back of the shed where she'd hidden it the night before. She estimated that she had about five minutes to get it out of the garden without her mum seeing. She unhooked the stiffened leather straps from the wheels and held the wing and propeller like a surf board as she quickly wedged it through the bushes. Then she went back for the bike and saw the continuing chaos in her house. Her mum looked like she had a bird's nest of her own on top of her head as she was waving her arms about, trying to shoo the pigeon out of the door. Mya had to move quickly as she could see some of the ducklings flapping out of the house and back into the garden. She jumped on to her bike and cycled right through the same gap that she'd put the wing through. Maybe she shouldn't race through this fast, she thought, as she was scratched on the arms by the bushes' prickly bits.

Mya continued to cycle but turned in the opposite direction to the Control Tower as Goose said there would be a wide path for the bike and the wing to fit down. Mya was thankful that it wasn't far as the brambles and shrubbery were getting too close together to cycle through. She left the bike on the open path and ran back for the wing so she could reattach it.

As she fixed on the wing she heard lots of little feet pattering along the path behind her.

"Okay, we're off," said Tails. "See you at the exam this afternoon." Mya's head snapped around but Tails had already disappeared with the other classmates and now it was just Goose and Plum Sauce wriggling in front of her.

"Ah yes," said Goose, staring at his feet. "I kind of forgot to tell you that we had our test flight with Officer Peacock the other day and she gave the all clear for our exam."

"Kind of forgot! Goose, it's the whole point of you teaching me to fly," Mya squealed.

"To be fair to Goose we got so excited about your plan to cause chaos in the house that it completely slipped our minds," piped up Plum Sauce, who had bits of potpourri all over her. It looked quite pretty.

"That's right," Goose said

excitedly, looking Mya in the eyes. "And now we've caused the distraction and you've got the bike out of the garden we can get to the field I was telling you about and get practising. Then you'll be perfect for the exam because it'll be fresh in your mind."

"I have to get off the ground first. Goose, this is a disaster."

"Star Catcher, you have a flying machine; you can do this. Now let's go and do some flying," Goose said with an excited squeak.

"Anyway you can't go back now," Plum Sauce chipped in. "Your mum will be grounding you for sure once she knows you've left with the bike. You might as well make the most of your last day of freedom." With that Plum flew down the path and Goose followed.

"C'mon, Star Catcher, this will be fun," Goose shouted back.

Mya hesitated but knew they were right. There was no point going back home. She had to try to get that pilot hat. She hopped on the bike and cycled after them.

Come fly with me

"This way will be much easier and it's close to where the exam will take place," Goose said as they rushed along the path and approached an open field. It was just the kind of space Mya needed. Mya didn't waste any time. She pedalled as fast as she could to the other side of the field. She wasn't getting off the ground but she was beginning to feel more comfortable on the bike. She could tell now how hard she needed to pedal to get it moving, and when she needed to brake. But she did fall off it several times as it would sometimes tip to the left or right and topple over. But she kept on trying. And then it happened. After an hour of cycling she found the right balance and speed to help lift her off the ground. She got so excited she forgot to carry on pedalling and came crashing down again. She worried that the wing might have got damaged but it hadn't. She just had a few scrapes and bruises on her knees, but she didn't care. She knew how to fly!

"Did you see that?" she shouted to Goose and Plum Sauce who were on the other side of the field.

She couldn't hear what they were saying but she could see them flapping excitedly and knew they had seen. She turned the bike round and went for it again. This time she got straight up in the air and wasn't going to stop.

It felt amazing. She was about two metres off the ground and she was flying.

"Star Catcher, you did it!" squeaked a little voice to her right. Goose had come to join her and was flying next to her. Plum Sauce joined her on the left. It couldn't have been more perfect – friends flying together with the wind in their faces. But now came the time to land the bike. She was coming to the end of the field and hadn't mastered turning yet.

"Remember, take-off and landing are the hardest parts and you've already conquered take-off," shouted Goose encouragingly.

Mya slowed down her pedalling and prepared to land. As she got lower and lower she gritted her teeth and squeezed the handlebars hard. The bike bounced on the bumpy field and she found herself in the air again for a moment before hitting the ground properly and coming to a controlled stop.

"Wow, that landing almost looked professional," squawked Plum Sauce. "I wish I could land as elegantly."

"Thanks." Mya was jumping for joy inside. She couldn't believe she had really flown and landed like a true pilot.

"Quickly, we'd better get the bike under cover and wait for our exam to start," instructed Goose.

"We can go watch some of the professionals if you like while we wait?" said Plum Sauce.

Goose waddled to the hedge at the far end. "If we leave the bike hidden in here then it's not far to the starting line in the next field, the one with the river running through it. We can all take our test, then you come flying over and amaze Lieutenant Drake. Me, Plum and Tails are the last three up. As soon as you see me leave, get on your bike and prepare to fly after Tails has gone."

"It sounds like you've got it all worked out," Mya smiled at Goose.

"Remember, you'll be the duck's quack at flying," Goose grinned.

Mya laughed, covered the bike and headed over with Goose and Plum Sauce to watch the show.

Like a bike over troubled water

Mya was crouching in the hedgerow with Goose and Plum Sauce watching the flights. She hadn't expected there to be such a crowd. She thought it would just be Lieutenant Drake and the ducklings. But it wasn't, it was a major event, with all the ducks and many other birds out for the day watching the air display. Various birds showed off their flying tricks over the river. A swift did a loop-the-loop while another swift flew directly through. Three red kites glided high above and took turns to dive down at the crowd and soar back up again to show off their speed and agility. The crowds loved it and cheered.

The show stopped and Lieutenant Drake approached the microphone.

"Friends and family," he shouted into it, "this is a very proud day for many of you as you witness your little ones fly for the first time. Like previous years, I ask that you all remain quiet while the exam takes place. You may cheer when each pupil reaches the other bank, and at the end of the exam."

Mya wished Goose and Plum Sauce good luck

as she watched them waddle over to their classmates to get in line. At the front of the line she saw Officer Peacock for the first time. She looked stern yet kind as she seemed to be giving the class some last-minute words of reassurance. Lieutenant Drake had finished his speech and was flying over to the other side of the river to the finishing line. Mya looked at the distance between the banks and estimated that it was about the same width as the length of the swimming pool where she went for swimming lessons. Which meant it was twenty-five metres wide. Mya gulped. She was going to have to work hard to keep in the air for that long.

The first duckling went to the starting line and once Officer Peacock gave them the go-ahead, he took off. He seemed very shaky at the start as he flew into the air and came very close to dipping into the water, but he made it across and all the birds cheered. One by one the ducklings took their turn. One got so nervous he misjudged the distance of the run-up and fell straight into the water before he even took off. But the rules stated they could have two chances and he managed to make it across the second time.

Eventually it was Goose's turn. Mya was desperate to watch him but she knew she had to get ready. She waited until he took off and it looked good. By the time she got to the bike she could hear the cheers so knew he'd made it.

"Ouch!" Mya shrieked. She looked down and was shocked to see Mr Sour pecking hard at her leg.

"I told you if I saw you again you'd be in big trouble," he said between pecks. "I thought the 'flying girl' might try and gatecrash one of our special events."

"Get off me, you horrible little duck. I haven't got time to deal with you." Mya kicked just enough to stop him pecking and heard the second round of cheers, so she knew Plum had flown successfully and Tails was up next.

"So, flying girl. Going to join the little duckling squad, are we?" he sneered. He had strange yellow bits flying from his beak and Mya thought he might be foaming at the mouth.

"Yes I am. And you aren't going to stop me," she stated defiantly as she edged her bike round him and got in the saddle.

"Be my guest. Let's see how well you fly, little girl. I hope it's better than when I saw you practising earlier. You'll never keep that contraption in the air for long enough. I hope you brought your swimming suit," he laughed from behind her. Mya was perplexed that he was letting her go without much of a fight and that he'd been watching her practise. But she couldn't focus on that, she had to get pedalling.

There it was, the final cheer: it was now or never.

She whizzed around the line of bushes and towards the starting line. The cheers stopped abruptly and were replaced by squawking and flapping as the birds panicked at the sight of Mya and her monstrous bike.

"Don't panic," she yelled as she zoomed by, nearly knocking a few birds out of the way with her wing. "I'm here to get my pilot hat."

She pedalled and saw Officer Peacock ahead of her, who stood her ground and looked at Mya quizzically. She didn't seem scared by her at all. She appeared to be trying to say something to Mya and pointed above her head, but Mya couldn't understand and there was no time to stop for a chat. So she ignored her.

As she pedalled on and reached the optimum speed and balance, she was worried to find that she wasn't lifting off the ground – and she was getting close to the edge of the water. The bike seemed to be dragging more than it did in the practice run. She looked across the river and saw the ducklings on the far bank flapping furiously. Then all of a sudden, Goose, Tails, and Plum Sauce were flying back towards her. What are they doing? Mya thought. The test isn't over yet. I thought they'd wait for me to get there. She pedalled harder and just as she got to the edge of the river she could finally hear what Goose was saying.

"There's a hole in your wing," he screamed. Mya looked up to the left and could see what he meant. There was a large hole at the end of her left wing and it was making the end of it droop downwards. She was off balance – no wonder she'd been unable to get in the air. The wing looked like something had pecked at it … and that something was most likely to be Mr Sour. That would explain the yellow bits flying out of his beak.

She closed her eyes and prepared to fall off the bike right into the water. It was going to be a freezing cold, wet end to her day. Mr Sour had won.

"I think you'd better keep pedalling, little girl. I can't do this on my own." Mya opened her eyes and was startled to see the water flowing past beneath her. She looked up and saw Officer Peacock had grabbed the end of the broken wing from above with her webbed foot which levelled the wing and gave her balance again. Mya pedalled as fast as she could. She wished she'd had some baked beans that morning to help with the speed but thankfully the wind was behind her and was helping to push them right over the river and across to the bank where the class awaited her arrival.

She didn't make the smooth landing she hoped for but the fact she landed on the ground instead of the water was good enough for Mya. She skidded along and the whole class had to jump out of the way before she could slow down and jump off the bike. Mya was elated: she'd made it. Amazingly the wing was still intact after the impact but now Mya could see how big the hole was that Mr Sour had pecked out.

Goose, Plum Sauce and Tails had flown back to the bank and joined the rest of the class. Lieutenant Drake flew straight over to Mya but completely ignored her and spoke to Officer Peacock who was standing beside her.

"Officer Peacock. You do realise this entry was not on the exam schedule?"

"Yes I do," replied Officer Peacock. "But when I saw her take off I couldn't let her fall into the water."

"Can I get my pilot hat please?" Mya interjected excitedly. Lieutenant Drake still refused to look at Mya.

"Officer Peacock, could you please let this civilian know that I appreciate her enthusiasm and determination but I cannot issue her with a hat as she was not on the schedule and her flight was assisted."

"WHAT!" screamed Mya. "I made it across."

"The rules state that all pupils must cross the river on their own to demonstrate they can fly independently. It's no good if you need another mallard to help you fly."

"But I would have done it if that rotten little duck Mr Sour hadn't ruined my wing," Mya raged.

At last Lieutenant Drake looked directly at Mya. "Dear girl, I cannot have you speak like that about my staff. That's a very strong accusation."

"It's true," came a small voice from the back. It was Goose. "Plum and I saw Star Catcher fly in practice and she's right, the only reason she didn't make it was because her wing was sabotaged. I didn't see who did it but I know Mr Sour has had it in for her since he saw her at the Control Tower." Goose snapped his beak shut as he realised he'd said too much.

Lieutenant Drake focused on Goose and the little ducklings.

"Goose, are you telling me this girl has been to the Control Tower? And that I've not been told of this security breach?"

Goose swallowed hard as he was unsure what to say next. The other ducklings, except for Plum Sauce, started uncomfortably shifting away. They didn't want to be associated with him when his punishment was handed out.

"Goose, I'm being put in a very awkward position here but we'll speak later. I need to speak with Mr Sour about this breach." He turned back to Officer Peacock. "But in the meantime I have to say I haven't seen this girl fly on her own and that is that."

Goose finally breathed out again as Lieutenant Drake would not be issuing any punishment just yet.

"What if you did see her fly?" asked Officer Peacock. "Give her a second chance and let her fly back to the crowd without any help. I can add her to the schedule." Lieutenant Drake looked at all the little eyes from his class staring back at him. He paused for a while before he spoke to Mya.

"That could work. You can have one more chance."

The tension in the air disappeared.

"Thank you!" Mya said gratefully. "I'll get the wing fixed and it should be ready for next weekend."

"Oh no. Today is the only day we do exams. If you can't do it now you'll have to wait until next year."

The tension returned.

"It's not possible to be ready now."

"I will give you fifteen minutes to get yourself ready and then you must fly back to the crowd."

"But—"

"That's my final offer. No more questions or pleas." With that he flew off back to the crowd leaving Mya speechless.

"It's a good offer," said Officer Peacock. "No human has even got this far before. Goose. Plum. Have a look for resources on this bank to help patch the wing. I have to prepare for our flyover. Good luck," she said to Mya, and flew off.

It's the final countdown

Mya was surrounded by a sad-looking winged bike and the rest of the ducklings who were padding around not sure what to do next.

"A good offer, indeed. I don't think so. He just wants me to fail," Mya muttered to herself as she lifted her bike up to inspect the hole. It was pretty big and small bits of polystyrene were still flying off. She kicked one of the tyres in frustration and carried on muttering to herself. "How dare that little Mr Sour Pants ruin this for me? I've worked so hard to get this far and I've still not got that pilot hat." She paused, looking at all the beaks pointing towards her and realised she couldn't give in now. "Okay, if he wants me to fly in fifteen minutes then I will, and I'll do it in style too."

"Star Catcher, that's the spirit, but let's not get ahead of ourselves," Goose interrupted – and then saw Mya's annoyance. "I mean, let's focus on getting the bike fixed so you can at least get over the river. Doing it in style will be a bonus." He trailed off, realising his pep talk hadn't come across as positively as he'd hoped. So he decided to get active. "We'll go and scan the bank for things to fill the hole like Officer Peacock suggested." The ducklings all followed Goose, and Mya reluctantly joined them, scuffing her feet as she went.

They searched all through the rubbish for over five minutes. "It's no good," Goose sighed. "I can't see anything here that will help. It's just plastic bottles, cans and empty crisp packets." He looked at Mya. "Maybe next year isn't such a bad idea," he said sheepishly.

Mya snapped at Goose. "Next year is a lifetime away. I can't wait until then." She softened her tone. "And anyway I want to get my pilot hat at the same time as you. As for that Mr Sour, well, he's just the meanest and we can't let him win now. Otherwise I'll just have to strap him to my back and he can fly us both over the river," she teased.

Goose giggled. "You mean like the first time you tried to fly with him when you fell out of the tree. 'Ooo my feathers, where are my feathers?'" Goose flapped around as he imitated Mr Sour.

Mya laughed at Goose and bent down to inspect some of the rubbish. "Hang on, this might work." She pulled out a tube of unused cling film. "How about we stuff the hole with the bottles after we flatten them out and then wrap the wing in cling film to hold it in place?"

"Sounds good to me," Goose agreed, thankful

that they had some kind of plan. He and the rest of the class gathered all the plastic bottles and began jumping on them to squash them flat. Mya found some string and selected the most flattened bottles to be tied together. She pulled them tightly and packed them into the hole in the wing. Once they straightened the wing and were in place she wrapped the cling film around the filled hole.

"You have two minutes remaining," came a distant voice from over the water. It was Lieutenant Drake on the speaker.

"Yes, yes," Mya muttered, annoyed by the added pressure of a countdown. Mya moved her bike into position and made sure she had enough runway before taking off. All the ducklings surrounded her to wish her luck – then waddled back quickly so she had the space to pedal without taking any of them out.

There was a slight downward slope on the runway so she used that to her advantage to get her speed up. Just as she reached the edge of the bank, and was worrying about a cold dip once again, the bike took off. It wasn't as high as she had been before and it felt a lot wobblier as the patched-up wing dipped slightly but she was in the air and clearing the water. Yes! But she had to pedal even harder as the wind was now against her, cooling her face and creating a slight resistance. It was definitely more exhausting this time. She could see the finish line but didn't know if she could make it. The bike began dropping a little and moved closer to the water. And her legs were starting to burn from all the pedalling she'd done that day. But then she looked at the crowd who seemed to be cheering and flapping their wings excitedly. She looked behind her and there were all the ducklings following her trail. They took their positions and fanned out in a V shape with Goose and Plum Sauce flanking either side of her.

"We thought you might need a little escort to help you do it in style," Goose shouted. Mya beamed. It was just the energy boost she needed. With the ducklings behind her, she spearheaded their display. There was no way she couldn't get to the finish line!

Hurrah! Made it! Mya gave a great whoop of elation as she cleared the line with just centimetres to spare. She landed with a thump and a skid and the repaired wing scraped all along the floor and eventually snapped off. She wouldn't be taking off on the flying bike again. This was its final voyage. She wasn't even sure if it would be useable as a normal bike any more. Her mum was going to go mad. But she was too exhausted to worry. She'd used up every last ounce of energy. She clambered off the bike, now on its side, and was greeted by all the little ducklings who swooped in to congratulate her. The Lieutenant waddled over and was about to speak when a sneering voice came from over his shoulder.

"You aren't seriously going to consider this stupid flying girl's entry, are you?"

Lieutenant Drake looked back at Mr Sour.

"I did promise the girl that if she could do an independent flight she would pass the exam."

"No thanks to you, Sour Chops," Mya shouted across.

"Star Catcher, a true pilot never loses their cool," Lieutenant Drake said to Mya. She was astounded he had considered her to be a true pilot. It was all she needed to calm herself down again. She had been accepted.

"Mr Sour, there have been some accusations flying around about you and this girl's wing. Now might not be the time to discuss this, but we must talk later."

"Oh no, we can talk now. Are you telling me that you're going to take the word of this imposter over your own fellow drake? What you need to be asking is, who has been helping this girl? There are traitors in your class. And I'm sorry to break it to you, I wanted to spare you the pain, but Goose and Plum Sauce have been giving her access to the Control Tower."

Lots of beaks in the crowd dropped to the floor, aghast at Mr Sour's claim. Plum and Goose looked mortified.

"They denied it of course, so I got them mucking out nests for the last week as punishment."

Lieutenant Drake looked at Goose and Plum. "That would explain why you've been so tired in my classes. Mr Sour, you can't just punish students with no evidence. And you know the rules: I must be consulted before any punishment is handed out."

"I cannot believe you're quoting the rule book at me! Yet you let this pretender take part in our exams. Call yourself Lieutenant? You're nothing more than a weak bill with broken wings." The crowd gasped at Mr Sour's ultimate insult.

Lieutenant Drake calmly waddled over to Mr Sour and spoke. "I was going to let you off by sending you for some top-up teacher training sessions, but I think you've showed me what a bad duck-egg you are and I don't need the likes of you influencing these ducklings. They need better role models even if that means allowing an enthusiastic human flyer to participate in the exams. Mr Sour, you are relieved of your teaching duties."

"Don't worry, Drake, I wouldn't want to work at such a lame-duck school. I'm delighted to leave." He shot a look at Mya who was still reeling from the shock of hearing Lieutenant Drake stick up for her. She knew Mr Sour was livid and didn't really want to leave, but he'd brought it on himself, so her momentary feeling of sadness for him quickly subsided, especially as he kicked her bike as he left the river bank.

"Well, class, I think that's quite enough excitement for one day, and there will be no more punishment. I think everyone involved has learnt their lesson while cleaning the nests," Lieutenant Drake stated without mentioning Goose or Plum Sauce. "We should get to the point of why we are here." With that another, older-looking mallard with dark brown and white speckled feathers, brought over a wicker basket full of individually wrapped pilot hats in an array of colours and designs. Lieutenant Drake asked the class to line up so he could present them with their hats. Mya stayed to the side, not sure if this was aimed at her as well. She looked at the basket again and realised that the hats would be too small for her.

"Star Catcher. Stop daydreaming and get in line please." Lieutenant Drake snapped her out of the despair she was beginning to feel. She moved silently to the back of the queue, still unsure how she was going to get the hat to fit. Plum received her pilot hat in light grey with contrasting deep red lining and black goggles on top. Goose stood proudly as he received his khaki green pilot hat, also with a beautiful contrasting red lining and goggles on top.

Then it was Mya's turn. Lieutenant Drake paused as he looked at the basket of hats customised for very small duckling heads. Then he rooted around and pulled out another khaki-coloured hat with yellow stitching around the googles and a silver grey lining.

"I thought you might need a bigger size," Lieutenant Drake smiled. "You've proved your worth, Star Catcher, now don't let me down. I want to see you flying those human metal boxes in no time. You have the passion and desire so make sure you go for it." Mya bent down so he could put the hat on her. It fitted perfectly.

Mya couldn't believe it. All the hard work had finally paid off. She wanted to hug Lieutenant Drake, but he seemed to anticipate that and stepped to the side clearing his throat. "Now, now, Star Catcher, none of that hugging stuff. Let's watch the show." He gave Mya a little wink. Mya grinned to herself and ran over to squeeze him anyway.

Just then the crowd, which had remained quiet through the ceremony, burst into applause as an announcement came over the speaker.

"And here we have the Yellow Bills display led by Yellow Bill One, Officer Peacock."

"Oh, wow, my favourite bit," Goose said to Mya as he looked up to the sky. Officer Peacock was leading the display of eleven Yellow Bills who formed the shape of a large bird in flight. Just as they shot over the crowd a stream of yellow clouds filled the sky behind them and hundreds of tiny parcels fell to the ground. The avian crowd scrambled to grab them. Mya looked down to ask Goose what the parcels were, but he was already darting across the bank to pick some up. He came running back with two in his beak and plopped them down at Mya's feet. "One for you and one for me," he said.

The two parcels glittered in the sunlight as the yellow wrapping paper caught the sun. Mya eagerly picked one up and opened it. Inside the wrapper was a small yellow pin. It was a V-shaped pin with three stripes sticking out on each side to look like wings and the initials Y and B engraved in the middle of the V.

"No way," Goose screeched as he watched Mya lift the pin up to her face. "Only one in every hundred boxes has a Yellow Bill pin."

"What's in your parcel, then?"

"The usual. Bird seed. Can I have a look at that pin?"

Mya could see the excitement in Goose's eyes. She bent down and showed it to him. Then she pinned it to the side of his hat.

"What are you doing?"

"You've been the best friend anyone could ask for and stuck by me through thick and thin. The very least I can do is give you this pin to thank you."

"No. You can't do that. It belongs to you."

"I can and I did. Besides, it suits your hat and it's already on there now."

Goose beamed. "Thank you."

"What will you do next?" Mya asked.

"Well, most of the Yellow Bills train in one of the cities for at least one month to build up their flying hours and reflexes, as it's so much busier to navigate. So I'm going to stay with family in London. It's a place called Clapton Pond. Apparently they have a lovely duck house with a fountain nearby."

"Sounds idyllic. But a month is a long time not to see you."

"Don't worry, my Uncle Puffin says a month is nothing and will flap by. I'll make sure to come and see you when I get back."

"You'd better. And next time I see you, it'd better be as a Yellow Bill." With that she squeezed Goose tightly and kissed him on the beak. She was sad he wouldn't be around for a while, but knew she'd see him again.

"At ease, Star Catcher," Goose teased as Mya's grip got a little tight. She got up and looked around at the amazing world she had been privileged to see. All the birds were busy opening parcels and hugging friends as they started to disperse. Goose was standing there gazing at Mya in a wiser, more confident stance than she had seen before. The pilot hat made him look more grown up.

"I'd better get home and face the music. Mum won't be happy I've ruined the bike but I'll think of something. And I can't wait to show my Uncle Arthur my pilot hat when he gets back from Singapore next week. He's going to be amazed."

And with that she picked up her battered bike, balanced the broken wing on the seat and pushed it along the riverbank, back towards home. She took one last look at the sky before leaving the path and watched as Goose and his classmates flew through the air with their pilot hats on, whizzing and darting over the river.